MW00460805

*Between the Devil
and the
Deep Blue Sea*

Copyright © 2022 Aletheia Morden

All rights reserved

Printed in the United States of America

First Edition, 2022

No part of this book may be reproduced or transmitted in any form or by any means, electronic or mechanical, including photocopying, recording, or by any information storage or retrieval system, without the written permission of the author, except for brief quotations embodied in critical reviewer or articles.

ISBN 978-7343827-5-4

Library of Congress Control Number: NRC109343

Published by Canyon Rose Prress
Benicia, California

email: info@canyonrosepress.com

Book design: Jan Malin

Cover image: the famous white cliffs of Dover, Kent, England
Cover Photography: Zora Zhuang

*Between the Dev
and the
Deep Blue Sea*

Aletheia Morden

What really happens, you know, never makes a good yarn. You have got to get an impulse from somewhere and then embroider it.

— William Faulkner

(From a letter postmarked March 13, 1925, *Thinking of Home: William Faulkner's Letters to His Mother and Father 1918-1925,* James G. Watson, Editor)

Table of Contents

A man finds refuge from caring for his elderly mother by making himself a new surfboard for Christmas.

The Rustle of Black Silk

During those dreary days of post-World War II when parts of England lay in ruins and refugees roamed Europe, my mother and I lived in my grandmother's house full of heavy Victorian furniture and stern portraits.

My mother went to work each morning as part of a much needed work force. Money was in short supply in most households. A lot of the population was dead; too many men had a jacket sleeve or trouser leg neatly pinned where a limb had once been. I longed to go to school, but at four years old I had to wait another year for kindergarten.

Mornings were for housework until eleven o'clock when my grandmother would announce: "Time for a dance." We'd put our dusting rags down, pick up the hem of our skirts, and skip around to music on the radio. Ivor Novello's *We'll Gather Lilacs In The Spring Again* was a waltz. Then it would be time for lunch before those long, dreadful afternoons.

In winter it would be dark by four o'clock. We'd sit in the

parlor: my grandmother in her high-backed chair next to the table by the window; me on an old kitchen chair with the legs sawn down so that my feet could touch the floor, playing with my doll by the fire. I loved the fire. Orange flames dancing in a frenzy, crackling and whispering secrets from long ago as the black coals turned red, then ashen gray while little yellow stars twinkled on the soot hanging down from the chimney flue.

My doll, Betty, loved it, too. She'd sit on my lap, nice and warm as the day shortened and purple shadows crept from the corners of the room.

Then a snap of starched white tablecloth being laid on the parlor table; the clatter of china plates and silver utensils, the whistle of the tea kettle in the scullery and the sound of boiling water pouring over tea leaves in the flowered teapot. My grandmother's footsteps fetching cheese and margarine from the pantry nobody had butter in those days.

Teatime!

She'd hand me a plate of bread and the long-handled toasting fork with three prongs. I'd impale a slice of bread and thrust it near the flames to toast as grandmother sat back down in her chair.

Soon, she'd start to hum, softly as first, then louder as she beat time on the tablecloth with the cheese knife.

And then, "Don't burn the bread, Emily," grandmother would admonish, my name lost as she summoned that of her little sister, long-ago grown and gone to Canada.

"Don't worry, Betty," I'd whisper to my doll. "It will be all right."

I kept my back to the room toasting slices of bread until

the plate was full, each piece a little blackened around the three holes where fork tines had been, evoking two eyes and a mouth. And then…and then…the swish of the baize curtain on its brass rail that led to the dark space under the stairs, the space grandmother had slept in every night during the war while bombs flew overhead, the space full of dark dreams.

"Musn't look," I whispered to Betty as *They* came into the room. A smell of faded violets, the rustle of black silk from great-grandmother's Victorian skirt as *They* glided behind me to the tea table. Grandmother had summoned her long-ago dead parents.

I had my doll and grandmother had hers.

And grandmother was very, very angry with her dolls. She listed their transgressions: *His* for drunkenness and neglect, leaving them penniless. *Hers* for abandonment of mothering. Grandmother shouted curses, screaming "you'll burn in hell" as shadows danced over the walls and sparks flew up the chimney.

I held my dolly tight. "Good girl," I whispered to Betty. "Don't cry."

And then…and then…the front door slamming, my mother's high heels tapping down the hallway, home from her typing job at Ocean Insurance. The rustle of black silk, the swish of the baize curtain, the smell of violets fading as grandmother put her dolls away. Silence in the parlor save for the ticking of the old clock. My mother entering in her business suit, switching on the light, patting her hair in place, sitting down at the table and smiling at us.

"What's for tea, then?"

The Queen of Tonga

We were watching Queen Elizabeth's coronation on our new television in June of 1953 when my father's relatives arrived, clumping up the stairs to our flat in my grandmother's Edwardian house. They were hours late. They'd missed seeing Princess Margaret riding in the glass coach, which wasn't made of glass at all. It was painted black and blue with a lot of gilt trim and big windows so the crowds could get a good view of the Queen Mother wearing the Koh-i-Nor diamond in her crown, one of the largest diamonds in the world. They'd missed the entire procession to Westminster Abbey through the streets of London where British Commonwealth soldiers, wearing their World War II medals, lined the route. Palace guards were wearing their beaver helmets and policemen their capes because it was a cold and rainy summer's day.

Most importantly, they'd missed seeing the Queen riding in the Gold State Coach with its carved and gilded mythical sea gods blowing conch shells, its dolphins, cherubs, lion's head and a sculpted crown on top pulled by eight Windsor Grey horses. I held a miniature souvenir of it in my seven-year-old hands, a fragile surprise gift from one of my mother's relatives, Aunt Bunny (whose real name was Elsa, but the British middle and upper classes used stupid nicknames in those days).

Ten minutes oration on the state of the weather went on behind me as the relatives struggled out of their wet coats and hats. They'd missed seeing the Queen enter the Abbey with her pages and ladies-in-waiting flanked by a long row of her personal guards on each side, white plumes on their steel helmets swaying in time as they slowly marched in their high black boots down the long aisle towards the altar, drawn swords pointed down by their sides.

The relatives had also missed news reporters informing us the ceremony dated from 974 A.D. and was now being conducted in English rather than Latin for the modern world-wide television audience of 277 million people.

They'd missed news tidbits such as Edmund Hillary and his Sherpa guide, Tenzing Norgay, being the first to reach the summit of Mount Everest, the event being New Zealand's gift to the new queen.

Over on the Korean peninsula we were told Canadian soldiers serving in the Korean war had libated the occasion with special rum rations and fired red, white and blue smoke shells at the enemy.

"What've we missed?" Great Aunt Mary asked seating herself in one of the chairs arranged in a semi-circle in front of the nine-inch black-and-white screen.

"Nothing much," my father replied, struggling with an armload of hats and coats. "It's on all day. Sit on the floor," he said to me. "Aunt Margaret needs that armchair."

I moved as directed, sitting cross-legged about twelve inches from the TV.

"Move!" Grandpa Albert and Uncle Stan roared in unison. "We can't see!

"Come and sit on the floor by us," Aunt Margaret said. She had my four-year-old cousin on her lap, spoilt Christine, who spied the little gold coach in my hand and wanted to play with it. I ignored her.

"Don't be so selfish," Grandmother Winifred admonished me. "Share."

Spoilt Christine made a grab for my new toy with her chubby little paws and promptly broke it.

I was heartbroken; I didn't have many toys. At school, I'd drawn a charcoal picture of the coach that had pleased me. I'd planned to add it to my own personal art gallery on the wooden walls of my playhouse, formerly known as my late maternal grandfather's photographic studio, also known as the garden shed. My teacher had had other ideas; she'd entered it into our town's exhibit of Coronation Art, and I never saw my drawing again.

"Go in your bedroom if you want to cry," my father ordered. "We're watching this." He had his eyes glued to the television screen as did his relatives now that they'd taken their seats. None of them had a television. My maternal grandmother had retreated to her son's house for a few days where the screen was larger and the armchairs more comfortable.

"I've put the kettle on," my mother announced. And so began the ritual of endless cups of tea and slices of my mother's fruit cake: tea so strong I was sure it would burn holes in the flowered chintz-covered armchair if you spilled a drop; iced fruitcake that did who-knows-what horrors to your intestinal tract.

Food had been rationed during World War II and for several years following. Dried fruit had come off ration in 1951, tea in 1952, and eggs in 1953. Sugar was in the process of coming off ration, so today's fruitcake was a special treat.

My mother had cut out little black-and-white head shots of the Royal family from the newspaper and propped them on the icing: Queen Elizabeth, her constantly complaining husband, Prince Philip, and the two Royal children, Charles and Ann, sat in a sticky row. Perhaps my mother thought they mirrored her own family since she always thought of herself as a princess, and we had added my brother six months before, making us a family of four. She and the Queen were born around the same time and almost shared the same name: Elizabeth and Betty.

And—final proof—my mother was fond of pointing to the veins in her wrist and declaring: "Look, blue blood." Or perhaps, as she told me decades later, married life was so boring to her after the excitement of being young and in uniform during World War II, my mother lived a parallel life to save her sanity.

With everyone's eyes on the televised ceremony as they sipped their first cup of tea—my mother had planned the fruitcake cutting for after the crown was placed on the Queen's head—spoilt Christine grew bored and restless. She wasn't interested in my baby brother, who lay in his pram sucking a pacifier dipped in sugar and watching everything going on around him.

"Christine, why don't you both go outside and play in the garden," my mother suggested looking out the window.

"It's stopped raining."

"I want to watch this," I protested.

My objections fell on deaf ears. Spoilt Christine liked the idea of playing in the garden and the relatives liked the idea of not having to listen to her whining.

I was disappointed, but made the best of the afternoon while fuming internally at my cousin. We played snail races along the garden path after rounding up every garden snail we could find from the lawn and vegetable plot; played chase in and out of my grandmother's fruit bushes until one of the snails got squashed underfoot and we had to conduct a burial service. Scooping out a shallow depression in the dirt, I nudged the unlucky snail into the hole with the toe of my shoe, dropped in a few blades of grass, then using the side of my shoe, covered the grave with soil while singing the children's hymn: *All Things Bright and Beautiful.*

When we started playing hide and seek, I sneaked back indoors when it was my time to hide. I'd done enough of my duty for the day.

On the television, Queen Elizabeth had been anointed by the Archbishop of Canterbury and was being crowned. A discussion about crown size was in progress amongst the relatives as the camera panned the Abbey audience: the women's were considerably smaller than the men's, Aunt Margaret noted. Men's crowns sat securely on their heads; the women's petite crowns perched on top of their heads "looking as if a woman put a foot down wrong, her crown would fall off," Grandma Winifred surmised. My father maintained the women wore smaller crowns because they had smaller brains. All the male relatives snickered, causing my mother to retort that since my father didn't have a brain, he wasn't qualified to say anything. Great Aunt Mary settled it by saying a lady's crown was smaller because it had to fit inside her tiara.

When spoilt Christine finally found me once more plunked down cross-legged on the floor in front of the screen, she started complaining that it was her turn to hide; the relatives insisted we go back outside.

"Can't we stay and play with the baby?" I suggested hopefully.

My mother shook her head. "No. We don't want to disturb him while he's being good."

Resigned to missing most of the coronation that day, I sighed and went back to the garden, my cousin trailing behind me. We played ring around the rosy for a while and then spoilt Christine made a beeline for my playhouse aka the garden shed. I barred the door.

"You're not worthy," I told her. She tried to push past me. I resisted. The time had come to make a deal.

"You can go in there if you let me go back in to watch television," I bargained.

She considered this for a moment, then pushed past me and tried to open the door.

"It's locked," I told her. "You need the magic key to get in there, but first you have to swear allegiance to a higher power. And let me go back inside and watch the coronation," I quickly added.

She stared at me with resentment, trying to understand what I meant, then capitulated. "Okay."

I retrieved the key with much ceremony from under a brick by the door and unlocked my playhouse.

Then I quickly ran back to the television. A glance at

the tea table showed the cake was gone. I'd missed it! Not a crumb was left on the cake plate. The relatives had eaten it all.

I'd also missed some of the procession from the Abbey to Buckingham Palace: Queen Elizabeth II in her golden coach, Prime Minister Winston Churchill, and some of the 129 monarchs and heads of state in their now-hooded carriages because the rain had become a downpour in London.

Our television may only have been in black-and-white, but the reporter described the scene in color for my eager eyes and ears. Roars of applause rose from the crowd as Canadian Mounties in red uniforms rode by on their horses; loud cheers erupted as Scottish bagpipers marched along in their kilts, and as two of four military bands playing the Australian National Anthem *("Waltzing Matilda")* and the Victorian marching song *("Soldiers of the Queen")* went down the Mall.

But the loudest cheers of all were for the Queen of Tonga, a monarch nobody had ever seen before, riding in the rain with her carriage top down "so the people can see me and I can see them," she told the newspapers. And the people loved her for it. Majestic Queen Salote Tupou III, six feet three inches tall and weighing three hundred pounds, laughed at the rain as she waved to the crowds.

The Queen of Tonga, the only other female monarch in the British Commonwealth, became the unofficial state attraction that day, wearing her crimson and gold gown covered with the silk mantle of a Dame Grand Cross of the Order of the British Empire, a tall red plume rising straight up in the air from her golden crown. She stayed almost dry, while her carriage mate, the Sultan of Kelantan, got soaked.

Queen Salote became a British favorite. Baby girls born that month were christened Charlotte (the English form of the Polynesian Salote); a racehorse was named after her; and more than one song was written about her, including "Linger Longer, Queen of Tonga."

The cheering crowds for Queen Salote almost drowned out the screams of spoilt Christine as she ran down the garden path from my playhouse. Her father went out to rescue her. It turned out my art gallery had terrified my cousin. Specifically, bright-colored crayon drawings of smiling relatives with very big teeth were just too scary looming over her from the wall.

Not my fault.

I turned back to the television, while the relatives fussed over Christine. My mother, stifling her laughter, whispered in my ear, "I saved you a piece of cake. You can have it after they all go home. It won't be long, now."

Midnight Mass

Christmas Eve, 1979. My mother and I are on our way
to church, our footsteps crunching softly on the frost and
snow as we walk down the lane arm in arm. There are no
sidewalks, just frozen ditches full of dead grasses and broken
bulrush stalks under leafless winter hedgerows, remnants of
a summer past.

The rising moon becomes hidden in low clouds as we
make our way past shadowed fields and barns. No streetlights
here; just a glimmer of light from an occasional cottage. Now
we are walking in the dark. We know our way from memory.
My mother is used to seeing in the dark, a crucial skill left
over from World War II necessary to get around at night. A
tiny orange glow suddenly materializes and I am startled to
realize someone I cannot see is silently passing us, smoking
a cigarette.

We reach the small cluster of buildings known as Ifield
Village, recorded in the Domesday Book of 1100 A.D., and

stop at the pub across from the church for a drink to warm us up. *The Plough* is filled with people having the same idea of making merry on a cold winter's night and so crowded that many of us sip our scotch whisky on the porch and benches outside, uncomfortable at first, but not for long as we stamp our feet on the trodden-down snow and empty our glasses.

The church bell starts ringing, summoning us to midnight mass. The crowd spills from the pub herding themselves across the lane through the lych gate towards the church door, hesitating for a moment on the threshold at the bright light and heat blasting out from inside.

"When did they put in electricity and central heating?" I ask my mother, remembering a darker, more damp church when I was young and it was easy to imagine Crusaders on their horses riding up to the altar for a blessing before their journey to the Holy Land and war: pay back to the Moors who'd invaded Europe centuries before.

"After last winter," she replies as we hastily squeeze into a pew. "Attendance had been going down for years."

Our little parish church soon becomes overfull. No room limit specifications here so it becomes standing room only for half the congregation. People are lined up against the stone walls several rows deep but continue pressing in, now crowding the flag-stoned aisle, which will make it difficult, but not impossible, to obtain the sacraments later in the service.

There are murmured apologies as people try not to bump into each other. The English translation of this actually means, "sorry for the invasion," as they accidentally touch. The English are sensitive about invasion of any kind, having become such experts at it over the centuries.

After singing the opening carol, our whole row sinks back

down to the pew en masse. We don't have much choice. The close proximity of neighbors' arms and shoulders pressing against each other literally pulls people on either side down. Likewise, remaining sitting when it's time to stand up again is not an option.

The clergy sit on chairs facing the congregants, almost touching knees with the front row. They're garbed in sackcloth-like vestments with lengths of coarse rope long enough for a hanging wrapped several times around their waist. What happened to the beautiful lace-edged robes worn over their cassocks with bright-colored sashes around their necks that I remember from childhood? It seems we're in the middle of another Reformation, this one concerning church garments. While the building has been updated to the 20th century, the people running it have gone back to wearing medieval costume. Or is that pagan?

As the service proceeds the church becomes a hothouse. People try to shed as much of their outerwear—coats, scarves, gloves—as discreetly as they can while trying not to put someone's eye out with an elbow.

I turn my head—the only part of my being I can freely move—trying to see if there's a temperature gauge somewhere on the stone walls near me, but there isn't. And, if there were, it would be impolite to shout out, "Turn the bloody heat down!" But I wish someone would.

People fan themselves with prayer books. My mother manages to reach into her handbag for a Mint Imperial hoping a burst of sharp peppermint flavor will keep her alert, then offers one to me, which I decline.

We joyfully start singing the last carol: "Hark! The Herald Angels Sing!" The man in the pew in front of us faints, but he can't actually fall down because there simply isn't room. His head slumps, his body sags, but he's held up by neighbors—until they have to sit and drag him back down with them for the Blessing.

I stifle a giggle as a suppressed shudder of laughter ripples around us. My mother frowns disapproval. The vicar makes the sign of the cross over his oxygen-deprived flock, eyes closed against the blazing lights, a sheen of sweat on his forehead.

The church doors are finally flung open. People stumble out into the freezing night air, dragging the now-reviving fainting man as everyone breathes deeply, putting on their coats and gloves before shaking hands and wishing each other a Happy Christmas.

The Frogman Cometh

In 1968 I lived with my lover, Roy, above the Santa Monica Pier merry-go-round in an apartment he had rented from Mrs. Winslow, the pier manager, for $12.00 a week. There were three rooms: a main room, a kitchen and a bathroom. Roy took the kitchen door off its hinges and propped milk crates under each end so we could use it as a dining table.

One night we hosted a dinner party. Spaghetti provided the main course, washed down with a half-gallon of cheap red wine. The entrée had been a tab of acid; dessert a fat marijuana joint passed around the table. Two candles stuck in empty Chianti bottles provided ambient lighting.

The sound of ocean waves gently washing onto the shore came through the open windows as Miles Davis' *Sketches of Spain* played on the turntable. Joe and Barbara, who also had an apartment above the merry-go-round, were our guests.

Joe worked as a hairdresser at Los Angeles' I. Magnin department store. Barbara had left her older, very rich husband to live with Joe. She was a model and wore beautiful clothes, although on this night she just had on an over-sized man's shirt barely covering her thighs. I wore a t-shirt dress that barely covered mine. Our lovers sported cowboy shirts and jeans as we sat cross-legged and shoeless on the floor.

Suddenly, the front door flung open. A dark figure stood in the doorway holding a gun, growling, "Hands up."

Was this a hallucination? We stared in stupefied silence as a man in a black scuba diving suit complete with skin-tight cap, goggles that almost covered his face and flippers, flapped his way into the room. He reached down and wrenched the remainder of the joint from Joe's fingers.

"Simon!" my lover exclaimed, as Frogman took a toke of the roach.

"Aw, man, how'd you guess," our next-door neighbor said, removing his goggles and pushing back his diving cap after he passed the joint back to Joe.

"The gun," Roy replied. "No one else I know has a Luger semi-automatic that his father took off a captured German submariner in World War II. Want some spaghetti?"

Simon tried to sit cross-legged, but it was hard for him to bend in the rubber suit and flippers. In the end he joined us at the table wearing…nothing.

Arthur and Larry

Part One: When Arthur Met Larry

Before the price of San Francisco real estate shot up into the stratosphere, Arthur and John bought a building on Oak Street in Hayes Valley. What had been three separate offices on three floors became three separate apartments: the lower one for Jeff and Joe, John's two brothers who'd come out from Wisconsin; the middle one for John, and the upper apartment for Arthur.

Joe was a Sherlock Holmes fan who watched Sherlock videos wearing his houndstooth cape and matching deerstalker hat while smoking his pipe. Jeff, an Elvis impersonator, had some specially-made Elvis-type jumpsuits. He wore white patent shoes and a black Elvis wig, and performed regularly at a club on Market Street, usually very late at night. By day he bagged groceries at Safeway down the street.

The brothers had bloomed after they moved to San

Francisco. Jeff become an honorary volunteer fireman and helped out at a mayoral candidate's campaign office. John cooked their meals and occasionally enlisted Arthur to keep an eye on them when he wasn't around.

Soon after they all moved in, repairs and painting started on the entire building. Each apartment was painted; a new roof was put on. Something always needed doing.

Larry was nursing a broken ankle in his apartment on the next street. One day, as he sat in his armchair by the window, he noticed increased activity going on in the Oak Street apartments. People were constantly coming and going carrying cans of paint and bags from the hardware store. Men wearing carpenter belts rebuilt back porches and stairs going down into the yard. Larry reached for his binoculars that he kept for bird-watching and trained them on the rear windows of Oak Street.

Every day something new was happening. Windows were being cleaned, new appliances were brought in. The third floor apartment was especially interesting: the guy rarely closed his blinds. Larry watched him hang his pictures, rearrange the furniture, place his knick-knacks just so.

One day as Larry reached for his binoculars and adjusted them, he saw another pair of binoculars looking back at him from the third floor window. Then came a message held up on a piece of paper: *what's your phone number?*

Part Two: Larry and Arthur Get Married

It was a lovely summer day when Larry and Arthur got married under the Rotunda at San Francisco City Hall. They'd waited twenty-one years, although same-sex marriage had been legal in California and other parts of the world for some time.

A lot had happened in the two decides they'd lived together. Life had been very good to them. They had moved out of the City and bought a new pied-a-terre in Oakland; renovated a weekend cottage up at the Russian River; gone cycling together; taken Spanish lessons (separately) and had had lots of holidays in Europe.

Arthur had taken up knitting and the art of making cocktails. Larry baked wholesome bread on the weekends that he toasted for hors d'oevres to accompany the cocktails. They both painted, but Larry also sculpted and rented an art studio on Guererro Street for awhile. Arthur still worked at a law firm in San Francisco, but Larry had changed jobs and obtained a Ph.D. Arthur's daughter, Daryl, had married and they had become grandparents.

Two weeks before Daryl and the two-year-old grandson were due to visit from Florida, Larry and Arthur decided over Saturday night cocktails to get married. They envisioned a low key affair on a Thursday morning.

Before long that idea morphed into a three-day celebration.

Friends and family were making plans to fly in not only from Florida and New York, but from Washington State, Colorado and Missouri before the official invites were emailed and restaurant venues decided upon. Life became a whirlwind of emails, texting and frantic searches on the Internet for a suitable restaurant.

In the end, Lynda never made it from Colorado and Aletheia and Ariel got stuck in Bay Bridge traffic and missed the ceremony. They went straight to the bar at *Absynthe* and waited for the wedding party to walk over from City Hall. Cousin Helene and her husband Louis, Arthur's brother David and his daughter Loren, Norma and her boyfriend, Daryl and her old school friend Bernie, and Grandson Colton sat down to a three-course wedding breakfast, along with John, who had married Rico a couple of years before.

The bridegrooms wore their best suits and sported matching gold wedding rings. Colton, was well-behaved and only broke one glass when he dropped his milk.

Afterwards, people drove north to the Russian River to continue celebrating. Larry made his special French toast on Friday for everyone who turned up at the cottage in the Redwoods for brunch. Arthur grilled hamburgers for Friday night dinner. People sat around on the deck under the tall trees and caught up on the intervening months or years since they had last seen each other. There was talk of a future holiday in Portugal and Southern Spain. Colton was a good boy and only misbehaved slightly—and not for long—with his harassed mother and grandparents. His Great-Uncle David took him to the beach for a break.

On Saturday evening the celebration moved over to

Spoonbar in Healdsburg where even more people turned up for conversation, cocktails and more good food. No dancing—although Colton tried his best to move around as wildly as he could before Larry picked him up. It's hard when you're only two feet tall and everyone else is so much bigger and drinking Vieux Carre's and Sleeping Beauties at the Garden Bar. Much better when everyone's sitting down to a banquet including grilled Spanish Octopus and Tuscan style flank steak, not to mention dark chocolate tort and yogurt panna cotta for desert.

On Sunday everyone went home and Larry and Arthur started planning their retirement.

A Little Murder

$\mathcal{B}$etty was cold. She sat in her living-room recliner looking through the sliding doors into the garden where a thin sun shone onto the flower beds. A trio of squirrels chased each other around the lawn and the rough trunk of the sequoia where they nested.

The caregiver, Maggie, had come and given Betty her morning wash, fed her breakfast and medications then left after tucking a blanket around Betty's knees and placing a cup of tea on the tray table beside her. But Betty was cold. Her son had turned the heat off after Maggie left then he had gone to work.

Betty was losing the power of speech and the ability to move by herself. She could press a button on the recliner to make it move up or down, forwards or backwards, but her hands were becoming stiff claws from arthritis. She gazed longingly at the cup of tea. That was difficult to handle, too. Why bother anyway? she reasoned, sighing as she watched the squirrels. There was nowhere she wanted to go any more, nothing she really wanted to do. Once upon a time, just a few months ago, she would catch the number 5 bus down to the seafront and go for a walk on the pier remembering all those years ago with her parents and later with her own children when they were small. Now, her mind was becoming empty. Now she slept a lot. Especially when she was cold.

Betty coughed. One of the squirrels broke off from the chase game and came over to the sliding doors. He peered in at her and sat there for awhile and they looked at each other. Betty loved watching the squirrels. Soon he ran off to join his friends as they all scrambled up the tree trunk for a nap. Betty took one, too.

When she awoke it was dark. She was on a stretcher being loaded into an ambulance by paramedics. Her son rode with her to the hospital.

"Chest infection," the emergency room doctor decreed as he scrolled through Betty's medical chart on the computer. He frowned. "Again. The third one in five months." He looked over at Betty and then at her son. "How much does she weigh?"

"Last doctor follow-up visit—eighty-five pounds," Betty's son replied.

The doctor typed his notes. "How old is she now?"

"Ninety-two," the son replied. "Nearly ninety-three."

The doctor nodded and closed out his screen. "Right. Antibiotics. We'll admit her and see how she does."

Betty died a few days later. Her daughter flew in from Australia to help make funeral arrangements. Stepping into the living-room she shivered and remarked: "Gosh, it's cold in here."

Between the Devil and the Deep Blue Sea

 *W*e're sitting in the Snuggery at Singing Hills Golf Club. Since I left home many years ago my mother and I have a life together on thin blue airmail paper, with my occasional visits back to England. This is one of those visits.

"I usually sit here and write to you while Dad plays golf," she tells me, pouring us cups of tea from a flowered teapot. My mother likes the Snuggery, which is anything but snug as it's the entranceway to the bar. It's mid-February and sunny, but there's a biting cold wind from Russia sweeping down over the hills bending Daffodils and Snowdrops into the hedgerow.

My father is not playing golf today. Sometimes, he tells me, his knees give out. And, sometimes, as he moves, I notice his knees bending slightly inward, so I know the cancer's gone into his hips.

We've driven across the South Downs at breakneck speed to get here for lunch. Some things never change. My father's driven that way for sixty-five years. He got his latest speeding ticket just a couple of months ago. Later on, I'll find or that he also wrecked the car on August Bank Holiday weekend when over 250,000 people turned up for Fat Boy Slim's birthday bash on Brighton Beach. Dad wasn't driving fast that day; someone else was.

We've taken a few minutes longer to get here today because he had to drive to the end of the lane first to point out a beautiful mock Tudor house, recently renovated. That's how he would like my parents' house to look—if there were time.

"They had to cut into the hill for the four-car garage that housed their Daimler and Rolls Royce," he tells me.

The place looks picture perfect, but the work was so extensive the owners ended up losing the house.

"It bankrupted them," my father states, twice, and then we speed off across the Devil's Dyke through the hills that lead to the golf club.

I had seen them at the airport before they saw me: two elderly people clinging to each other, much paler than they used to be, and walking slowly. He carried her handbag. She's afraid of lifting anything in case she has a heart attack or stroke. She's thin; he's not any more. It's the meds. They've made him put on weight and now he resembles his mother, Winifred, at that age. Out of her six children, he was her least favorite.

"He's a lot like his father," she used to say.

The story goes that Winifred's childless sister, Mary, and her husband, Harry, had wanted to adopt my father when he was a child.

"But what would that have looked like to the neighbors?" Winifred confided to me. (My father's loss of the perfect childhood—Mary and Harry owned a sweet shop in London.) I had to call across the airport *Arrivals* section several times to get their attention. They were almost two hours late to pick me up, but I didn't mention it. After we hugged, they started arguing about where they'd parked the car, but it's not really an argument, it's the way they've always communicated. Some things never change. My mother looks stylish in her long, navy blue wool coat and velvet hat, a shocking pink scarf around her neck, which he insists is red.

He's lost several teeth, and I have trouble understanding him at first. "Why don't you get a bridge?" I suggest.

"If my check-up's okay in July, I will," he replies.

Everything looks the same to me as we speed along the motorway. This could be Northern California in winter, but it's Southern England. The old Georgian houses are till there, the rows of centuries-old farm cottages, except they now have a concrete barrier to protect them from the SUVs speeding past.

My mother chatters on about how everything's changed: the airport getting larger by the minute, but I am still surprised by endless woods and farmland that stretches all the way to the coast. The way it always did. The motorway snakes across the Downs. It wasn't built the last time I visited my parents, but now it looks as if it's been here forever. And now, forty-eight hours after I've landed, I feel as if I've been here forever.

"The Nazi" at Singing Hills Golf Club comes over to ask if everything's all right once we have ordered lunch. I am introduced. My brother calls the concierge "the Nazi" because she threw him out of the Snuggery once for wearing jeans. Jeans are *not* allowed at Singing Hills. I am in black jeans, but the Nazi doesn't seem to notice. Perhaps it's because people are not wearing black jeans in England at the moment. Everyone wears blue jeans; the same shade of blue. No faded, no stone washed, no light, no dark, just—the same shade of blue.

After the concierge in her nav-blue suit and Italian silk scarf moves on, my father gives me the gossip: A few years ago, a businessman who was developing golf clubs in England in concert with a Japanese company was convicted of fraud and went to jail.

"I think this is one of his places," my father confides, "and I think that's his daughter."

I must remember to relate this tidbit to my brother.

My parents are good at telling stories; they just have different styles. My mother can't stand too many stories unless it's one of hers, so she immediately changes the subject to tell me about a recent time they were on television at their dance club in Hassocks. My father fills in if she misses a point.

"We didn't know they'd be there," he interjects, and I get the impression my mother's talking about a local interest story on the news regarding elderly people and dancing.

"Nice lads, with a TV camera," she adds. "They were filming all around our feet. Dad kept swinging me out, and my skirt kept twirling around."

"They kept filming down low, around our feet, and then," my father pauses dramatically, "I realized, Oh, Christ! I'm wearing brown shoes with gray slacks." For some reason, he thinks this is hilarious.

They both missed seeing the program when it aired on television, so a friend lent them a video of *The Hassocks Tea*

Dance Murders.

"You could tell it was us," my mother says. "And we were on the screen quite a bit. My dress looked good as Dad kept swinging me out."

The Hassocks Tea Dance Murders? In a letter last fall, my mother mentioned a program called *The Girl Who Got Away.* But perhaps that was another program because neither of them pay any attention when I mention the discrepancy.

"It was based on a murder case in the 1970s," my father explains. "This man was having an affair with a woman, and her husband got jealous and stabbed him. They caught him because they'd both been seen at a tea dance in Hassocks."

I personally think the nice lads with the camera exploited the elderly. "Did you sign a Release?" I ask.

"They were from the BBC," my mother says as if this explains everything.

"Did they pay you?"

My parents look confused for a split second, and then move on.

"It wasn't very good," my father sums up. "But, strangely enough, I looked just like the fellow who got murdered."

And that's the end of this story as my mother switches to one about her trip to Brighton General in the middle of the night. This is the hospital I was born in which is located on one side of a hill that forms part of the vast South Downs. Brighton Racetrack sits at the top of said racetrack favored by my maternal grandmother and grandfather in their day, with a cemetery on the other side where both grandparents are buried.

It had been a busy night in the ER, my mother explains, so the gurneys were lined up in the hallway. One young man was a motorcycle crash victim who was covered in blood and crying. My mother, in spite of being in the middle of a heart attack, felt compelled to comfort him.

"I leaned over and took his hand because he was frightened."

She then startles me by acting out both roles from her armchair in the Snuggery, complete with different voices.

"I'm going to die!" (Victim)

"No, you're not." (Mother)

"I am!"

"They'll get to you."

"I'm dying!"

"You're not dying, they're taking care of you."

My father chimes in. "Which one was that, the one with the long hair?"

"Yes, the one that looked like Jesus."

And here the story starts to meander, and my vision of the scene fluctuates between seeing my mother leaning over the young man from her gurney like some sort of Mary Magdalene, or, like some sort of Jesus figure healing the sick. This seems strange to me because in my childhood memories my brother and I could be vomiting on our bedroom floor in the middle of the night and my mother wouldn't budge out of her bed. When I was five, she nailed a picture of Jesus next to my bed and told me if I felt upset I should talk to Him.

But now there are changes. I notice a kinder, gentler religious tone in my parents' conversation. God is referred to as "Our Lord," and Jesus is sometimes referred to as Jesus, but sometimes as "Our Lady." I am momentarily confused. I grew up with a more "Passion of the Christ" scary, violent viewpoint of religion that caused me to be wary of Christianity, and turned my brother into a Marxist.

As we eat lunch, my mother moves the story on from being in the ER to being admitted into a hospital ward for a few days. And this is where the bickering really starts between my parents. Over a dead body. Specifically, the man in the bed across from my mother, who was alone when he died.

"No, he wasn't, his family was with him," my father insists.

I presume he was visiting my mother at the time, although I daren't interrupt for such a teensy particular.

"They'd been gone for hours, the nurses had to call them back," she reminds him.

"He had people all around him."

"No, he didn't. He lay there by himself. Then he turned gray, so I knew he'd died," my mother insists.

On and on they go as we eat a lunch of prawn sandwiches. The same thing happened yesterday on the way back from the airport. It was my mother's birthday, and since we were going out to dinner that night, she hadn't wanted a big lunch, "just a coffee."

We stopped at Middlebrook farm to pick up a loaf of wholesome bread. I offered to pay, and that's when my mother decided she wanted lunch.

"You'll regret this," my father advised as we ordered from the farm's restaurant.

I guess he was right, because my mother had to sit at four tables before she finally found the right one. There were too many people in the place, and too many children having a school holiday, even though the restaurant was nowhere near full.

"It's usually empty," my mother kept repeating, but she didn't want to leave.

Once we sat down, my father took a turn criticizing the people at the next table. A woman had asked the waitress if she could have one of the unopened yoghurts someone had left behind at another table, rather than waste it by having the staff throw it away when they cleared.

"Paul hates that kind of thing," my father said. "He'd never do anything like that. Would you?"

I'd only been in the country a few hours, but recognized this as one of those minefield questions, an entrée into comparing my brother and me. I made a neutral noise and started eating my lunch. This was a wise choice because my father then orated for several minutes on other people's bad behavior.

Now, my mother needed attention. She started whining about the seasonal, organic vegetables they served her for lunch, as if they'd done it on purpose. ("I don't like parsnips; cauliflower gives you arthritis.") And, yes, she pouted.

When the overworked high school-age waitress substituted a salad, my mother complained she didn't like coleslaw, or *that* kind of lettuce. My father criticized the kinds of lettuce on her plate that she didn't. and they argued over baby greens as the waitress beat a fast retreat.

My mother then found her meal cold. My father stated what a waste of money it was to pay for cold food, even though it was my money, not his. Strangely enough, my food stayed hot the whole time I was eating. My mother voiced displeasure at having coffee *with* the meal instead of *after* (my fault), and retrieved a biscuit from her handbag while she poked around the food on her plate with a fork.

When I was a child, I found this arguing in public

embarrassing. Since I've been out of the house for decades I find it mildly interesting, like some awful cabaret. It fascinates me how they can argue over what lousy food it is here since the chef changed, and what personal offenses the kitchen staff were committing by bringing out containers of food and dishing it up to the line of patrons as fast as they could *without hot plates underneath* all the while drinking beer (him) and hot coffee (her) without choking.

"Die already," flitted across my mind.

Would every meal be like this? Well, yes. Here we are at Singing Hills not forty-eight hours after I've landed, and I realize what game this is. As long as they're arguing, I am safe. If I say anything specific or take sides they will join forces and turn on me. At a minimum I will be accused of interfering, causing conflict, starting an argument. I will be the bad one, the trouble-maker.

However, that hardly applies any more. Things changed when my sister-in-law came on the scene. I was the bad one, the one that got away (thousands of miles). Then Geraldine inadvertently stepped in and replaced me. She suspected something, but she didn't quite get it, and she still doesn't. Over the years, because of her (normal) behavior, she's become the bad girl, and I've become—the Golden Girl.

As we sit in the Snuggery finishing our lunches, my parents are still arguing about the hospital, but they've moved on from the dead body and back to the young man. Although, now, somehow, there seems to be two young men in distress on their gurneys, and there's confusion on my father's part as to which one my mother's talking about.

"Which one?" he demands.

"The other one," she says.

"Which other one?"

"The one with the long hair."

"They both had long hair."

I cannot help myself. "The Jesus one," I say.

And then my mother laughs, a strange rasping sound, like the sound of someone not used to laughing any more. Everything stops as my mother laughs and laughs and can hardly catch her breath. She once confided to me that sometimes she hated herself, and now I know what it is she really wants. She wants to be healed. She wants to be healed from herself, from being who she is in this life: her guilt, her fears, her disappointments; her body in all its imperfections—the face God gave her, the shape of her nose, her hormones and arthritis; her dislike of being touched, or touching anyone else; longings—unfulfilled; the inability to control people and things around her: the war, her father's death, her mother's, brothers' and lovers' deaths; broken engagements; betrayals—hers and others; fantasies and depression; anger, grief and sorrow; lack of validation and feeling trodden on by life. Being a woman. Her 80th birthday. My mother wants to be healed from being human.

Catkins twist on their branches in the icy wind outside the window of the Snuggery. Purple crocus push through the earth. Daffodils and Snowdrops bend into the hedgerow. One thing that has changed: spring flowers seem to grow closer to the ground than they used to.

The Last Ride

*M*um and I are riding the number 5 bus down to the seafront. The number 5 is a double-decker colored red and cream that's been unchanged since my childhood. We sit up top in the front row, swaying slightly while the bus gathers momentum as it glides through the town. Mum sits next to me in a little plastic baggie in my handbag. Or part of her does.

Part of her has already been sprinkled on the South Downs, the range of hills that rise up from the ocean in a steady slope continuing past the beach, through the town of Brighton to beyond where there's a steep drop-off and a view for miles and miles over the countryside.

That range of hills along the southern coast of England once had beacons placed all along it hundreds of years ago that could be lit if invaders were coming across the English Channel. If, for instance, the Spanish Armada was spotted, the beacon torch flames could be seen a great distance away northwards across the countryside towards London. Riders would then jump on their horses in tandem for the rest of the journey, taking the news to Queen Elizabeth I, who would mobilize the army which, in turn, would rush towards the coast and be ready to repel the enemy on the beaches.

The beacons have long since been done away with, but the remains of a Roman camp from an invasion hundreds of years prior to the Elizabethan Age can still be seen a few streets from where I used to live. It always looked like a few grassy mounds surrounded by a spiked fence near the tennis courts and children's swings to me, but you can't argue with that kind of archeologically documented history.

The Downs was the second thought for Mum's final resting place. My father had been sprinkled in the church garden, but this was currently in the middle of a renovation when we got there. My brother searched in vain for the particular red rose bush that Dad's ashes had been chosen to fertilize a few years before, but as we gazed at the piles of excavated dirt and upended turf, the rose bush had obviously been tossed out along with all the other plants and shrubs. So much for today's reverence with any nod to the more recent past.

We stood on the pavement wondering what to do next: me holding mum's box of ashes; my brother worrying about where we'd left the car with the parking meter running out and the inevitable issuance of an expensive ticket by the ever-vigilant and just-waiting-to-pounce Brighton Police. Fortunately, I thought of a better place other than the moldy old church.

Mum always loved to ramble across the Downs with her father when she was a little girl in the 1930's. These walks were frequent since he had a weak heart and the exercise was good for him. Since he was 'a gentleman' he also didn't work, but had a small monthly stipend from his mother's estate. My

grandmother supplemented the family income by turning
their home into a boarding-house during the summer. There
are black-and-white photographs of guests sitting in deck
chairs in the back garden smoking cigarettes and posing for
my grandfather's camera. My uncle's childhood memories
included catching pigeons for dinner in that garden until my
grandmother thought up the boarding house idea.

The house was sold long ago after my grandparents died,
but not much else has changed since then regarding the
Downs. You can walk along the hills from Brighton to Lewis,
the County seat, through miles of wildflowers in summer,
and flocks of grazing sheep and cattle all year round, which
is why I had a hard time finding a clear space of grass upon
which to sprinkle Mum. The Downs are full of wildlife: rab-
bits and foxes, stoats and weasels. Along with the domestic
livestock they leave scat everywhere. And, of course, people
walk their dogs there. The hills are covered in shit. You have to
tread very carefully when you step off the footpath, although
mountain–bikers don't seem so fussy about clean tires.

My nephew's Australian fiancée fidgets and shivers in
the cold wind as I look for a clear space for Mum. As much
as my mother and I were at odds with each other my whole
life long, I simply cannot bring myself to just dump her in a
cow pat. It does not escape my notice that her beloved son,
her favorite child, doesn't seem to care. He just wants me to
get on with it.

I finally find a small clear area on the much-nibbled grass
and open the box, first removing the little certificate underneath the lid stating the name and death date of my mother.
You can dispose of someone's cremated remains anywhere
in England as long as you are accompanied by that little

certificate clarifying who and what the sandy grains really are.

My mother was really small, weighing eighty-five pounds by the time she died, but there seems to be a lot of her as I squat down and tip the box close to the ground. There's a fierce wind blowing and I don't want her to end up all over us. I say a silent goodbye prayer as the white sand that is now my mother settles in a little grass and dirt hollow, then gradually drifts across the landscape.

"Let's go," my brother says.

We're all cold now and want to get back to the warmth of the car, but the box is far from empty.

"We can sprinkle the rest of her among the plant pots on the patio," my brother says impatiently. "Then I can sit out there and talk to her,"

Oh-kay. But I'm hatching another plan. Which is why Mum and I are taking the bus ride to the beach. Nobody but me knows about this. Nobody cares anyway, which is why I haven't mentioned it out loud. I want my own thing without interference or comment from anybody else. I want mother-daughter time. I want closure. In my heart, I know Mum would approve. She was very big on privacy. No one will miss this little bit of her. The box containing the residual quantity of Mum's immortal self, currently resides on a shelf in her bathroom. My exclusive portion of her is in the Ziploc baggie in my purse, the legally-needed certificate alongside just in case, as the bus rattles along past the shops and towards the sea.

It's raining by the time we get off the bus by the pier. No worries. I unfurl mum's purple umbrella which immediately blows inside out from the stiff breeze. The ocean hurls white-capped waves onto the stony beach, bereft of any other living thing as the rain pours down harder. No worries. No witnesses. I can definitely do my thing in private.

Mum loved to walk along Brighton pier for almost ninety of her ninety-three years. First, with her mother and father and other family members and friends. Then with me and my daughter. Mum lived in this city most of her life. Once, when she was discussing end-of-life arrangements with my reluctant brother, she finally burst out with, "Well, you can just fling me off the end of the pier, then." It was indicative of the type of statements she would make, but didn't really mean, and in response to my brother making the mistake of nixing her idea of something short of a state funeral.

I had no intention of opening the plastic baggie and releasing her at the end of the pier. Just a last short walk along the wooden boards, I'd thought, seagulls crying overhead and gentle waves lapping at the shore as Mum and I take our last stroll and relive some pleasant memories. Not going to happen now in lieu of the current downpour, so I cancelled those thoughts and looked along the promenade to the right. The beach stretches all the way to Hove. It's on that side of the pier we always favored to swim from when I was growing up. I briefly envisioned myself walking along to the part I remembered and sending Mum off from there, but it's too far to walk in this weather. I glance to the left side of the pier. Much closer. That part of the beach will have to do.

I walk past the Brighton Aquarium which I've never been to, and what used to be the Florida Ballroom, which I have. In the early nineteen sixties it was a Mod dance place which played all the latest records for teenagers. It was the dance hall where I first heard the Beatles' mega hit *Love Me Do*. The crowd roared for the disc jockey to play it over and over again. And he did.

Down the steps from the promenade and cliff face to the beach I go, very carefully crossing Volks Electric Railway line, a narrow gauge heritage railway and historical Victorian seafront attraction. First opened in 1883 the trains now supposedly run only in summer from Black Rock—once vast tidepools, now a marina and shopping center complete with a cineplex—to the pier. My grandmother took me for a ride there and back once when I was very young.

Although it's October, so ostensibly no trains are running, I still look both ways before I open the mesh crossing gates and carefully cross the tracks along the top of the beach. Silly I know, but an ingrained lifetime habit that comes from navigating busy main roads while walking to school without the benefit of zebra crossings or traffic lights when I was five years old. I learned to be careful at an early age. Nasty things could happen to little girls. Nowadays, I still don't want any surprises. And I don't want to possibly be electrocuted. One never knows. Life can be surprising at the oddest moments.

Mum's goodbye ceremony is pretty brief as I'm trying to balance the umbrella and deal with the Ziploc baggie in a raging wind at the same time.

"This is the best I can do," I say tipping out the grains of her onto the pebbles and watching the waves take Mum away for her last swim. "Maybe it's not the side of the pier you considered as upscale as further along towards Hove, but heck, it's the same sea. Besides, you always reminded me that life's not perfect. Bon Voyage, Mum. Thank you."

I sit there under the umbrella in the rain for a while, watching the waves take her farther and farther from shore. She always loved swimming in the ocean, said it was restorative, although she nearly drowned when she was 80 and a strong current took her further out than anticipated. A 10-year-old boy saved her.

Mum was religious, couldn't wait to lay herself at the feet of Jesus, she always said. As I gaze toward the misty horizon I contemplate that if He really did walk on water, Mum might be gazing up at Him right about now. But I'm getting cold, and the afternoon is darkening. Time for me to go.

Later that evening as I'm sorting through the old photos, I come across a black-and-white snap of my mother taken at the beach when she was about six years old. She's dressed in a bathing suit, holding her dolly up for the camera and her father, who was a master photographer as well as a sometime actor, and later a Downs walker. Little girl Mum is smiling in the sunlight, her bucket and spade on the beach beside her. And suddenly I see it, the pier in the background, and I realize from the angle that the photo was taken that it's the same side of the pier, just about on the same spot, where I had released her to the ocean that afternoon.

Bon Voyage, Mum. Godspeed.

By the Wind, Sailor

Drifting is the most economical way to travel the vast waters of the world for jellyfish. It takes little energy for them to gently pulse their bells and ride the ocean currents.

One morning in Venice Beach, California, Gary Edwards was inspecting the tideline. After a rain storm the sea has super fast hollow waves. Surfers were out in full force developing quick turns and cutbacks, aerial floaters and power slides as they directed the elements of air and water and their bodies toward one perfect moment, one perfect ride. Gary stood at the door of this intense gravity and raw forces of nature and decided against going in. The water was also full of run-off from the storm drains of Los Angeles.

He sighed and turned to walk back across the beach. Passing Lifeguard Station 38 he saw a broken surfboard lying on the white sand.

"Whose is that?"

The lifeguard shrugged. "Who knows?" It's been there all morning."

Gary nodded. The sea spit up all kinds of things after a storm. Crab shells crushed by thrashing waves; strings of mussels torn from rocks; bird claws (*someone's tiny foot*). And then there were yards of styrofoam cups from hundreds of takeout windows and gourmet coffee shops; tennis balls and condoms; broken beer bottles, and plant clippings from a thousand gardens in Los Angeles.

Gary picked up the broken board and took it home to the little white house on Ocean Front Walk where he had lived ever since his parents brought him home from the hospital after he was born.

His elderly mother, Lillian, was in the back garden inspecting her flowers. She'd just washed her hair. As she moved around the yard the morning breeze gently ruffled and lifted it like big white sails around her head. She stopped and stood still in front of an old bathtub filled with Cosmos for quite some time.

Gary came through the side gate carrying the surfboard. "Look what I've found," he called, but she didn't turn round, and he realized she wasn't wearing her hearing aid.

Suddenly, Lillian flapped her arms. Then she waggled her fingers. At first, he thought it was some sort of ritual for the flowers to grow, but then he noticed her red fingertips. Lillian was drying her nail polish after a manicure.

"Mom!" Gary said, standing beside her.

"Eh?" She turned round sharply.

"Look at my Christmas present."

"Oh," she said, glancing at the surfboard, then back up at him to see if he was hurt.

"I found it on the beach."

"Ah!" She was relieved he wasn't injured. "I think I'm ready to go back to bed."

"I'm ready to eat," Gary said. "Do you mind if I don't change my clothes?"

After breakfast, and after Lillian had gone back to bed, Gary dressed in his late father's white surgeon's coat, a white hospital mask, and an old white cotton beach hat someone had once dropped on the boardwalk. He moved his car out of the garage, got two trestles from the garden shed, and laid out the broken surfboard. It had already been hosed off and left to dry while he ate his cornflakes. Gary pulled on a clean pair of white cotton gloves and slowly ran his hands over the board, noting all the imperfections and dents. It had brownish patches here and there as if it had been beaten up, kind of like manatees when encountering power boats. Gary liked manatees.

He went back to the garden shed behind the garage and retrieved another old surfboard, which he laid out beside the one already on the trestles. Gary dug out a metal tape measure from his surgeon's coat pocket and carefully measured both boards, making pencil notes on the back of an old tides chart booklet. Then he revved up his chainsaw and cut off the jagged and broken parts from both surfboards, being careful to leave the fin on the second board exactly where he wanted it; a fin placed an inch one way or another made a big difference when riding a wave.

All week Gary worked on his new surfboard. He joined and glued the two parts together and smoothed the surface. He placed a strip of paper left over from painting the kitchen windows around the board creating a paint sealant line. Then he painted one side of the board with three coats of resin. As each coat dried the resin dripped over the edges, hanging down in stalactites, which he sanded off.

Just before applying the last coat, Gary placed a personal logo on the front of his new board. He'd gone out on his bike early in the morning on trash can pick-up day. People who've lived in Venice a long time carefully place their trash out: what they can't use any more someone else might want, whether it be a neighbor or a homeless person. Unwanted clothes and household items are placed next to the trash cans or hung on the fence the night before trash pickup day. Such items usually disappear well before morning. Since it was just after Christmas, Gary Edwards reaped a bonanza of small appliance boxes. He carefully cut the "GE" symbol from one of them and glued it onto his new surfboard. The rest of the boxes he stashed away for future use.

New Year's Eve came and went. Gary and his mother celebrated quietly and were in bed by midnight. He was up early the next morning, inspecting his board.

His neighbor, Stella, came over to take a look. Gary shoved a block of surf wax he'd found on the beach under her nose. "Smell this."

"Coconut," she said. "Mnnn."

"Smells so good they have to put a warning on it," he told her. DO NOT EAT was written on the side. "I usually find it on the beach. They all have different smells because there are different types for different water. Santa Monica Bay is cool water. The tropical water stuff smells different."

Stella admired Gary's handiwork on the new surfboard.

"It weighs seventeen pounds—I weighed it on the bathroom scale—and it's nine feet eight inches long, three feet shorter than my regular board."

"Isn't that kind of long?" Stella didn't ride boards; she body surfed.

"Short boards are for cutting up the waves," Gary informed her. "Long and wider boards are for paddling."

Lillian came out of the house with a tray containing glasses of POG for them both. She'd acquired a taste for the passion fruit, orange and guava juice mix during a stay in Hawaii.

"Happy New Year, Stella! "Did you have a nice Christmas?"

"I did." Stella handed her a box of chocolates, which Lillian placed on the tray.

'I'll save these for later. My medications keep me up at night."

Just then the outside telephone rang and Lillian went to answer it, adjusting her hearing aid as she walked towards it. Gary and Stella could hear her emitting beeping sounds all the way across the garden.

"It's Sam, Gary!" she called over. Sam was Gary's older brother.

"Tell him 'hi' from me," Gary shouted back. His mother was already deep in phone conversation.

"She's ready now." Gary gave the surfboard one last rub with the wax. "I think I'm gonna take her out."

"See you, later." Stella finished her juice and placed the empty glass back on the tray. "Enjoy your ride."

Gary stood at the edge of the sand watching little ripples of water roll in and break over his feet. Waves are born at the south pole fueled by the sun streaming down from above as they're driven across the planet by the wind, the molecules traveling in a circular motion bringing up nutrients from below.

A flock of surfers sat offshore like mullahs on prayer mats silently facing the horizon, watching the imperceptible swell of the ocean. Brown pelicans glided low over the water looking for something to eat. Gary glanced to his right where the ferris wheel on the pier stood out against the green and purple of the Santa Monica mountains. It was a beautiful day. But not for surfing.

Oh, well, Gary thought. *She's a longboard, anyway. I'll take her for a paddle.*

He waded into the ocean and pushed off, then turned away from the other surfers, floating parallel to the shore, down towards the breakwater. People were fishing from the rocks, playing frisbee on the beach, visitors from faraway places with backpacks, but no shoes or socks, strolled along the shore. Gary had never gone anywhere east of the Mississippi. His brother had left for college in another state and never come back. He had a large family now, and lived far away. Gary had attended the local college, but when his father had died someone had to stay with his mother and take care of things. He'd had a girlfriend once, but she hadn't liked him going surfing all the time.

"You don't know what it's like," he'd told her. 'Being inside the water. The sun's reflection makes the world a beautiful shade of blue."

A small wave came along, hardly a wave at all. This might be as good as it's going to get for right now, Gary thought, and stood up on his board. He almost fell backwards, but saved himself to ride the two hundred yards into shore. He didn't have to bend and twist to stay afloat, he simply stood still and let the wave support him all the way to the edge of the sand. For Gary it was the perfect wave, the perfect moment. It was the moment he walked on water.

How you interpret the nature of God cannot be regulated or ordained. How you acknowledge the nature of God is up to you. The world is always at prayer.

Acknowledgements

Many thanks to the Wednesday Novelists Circle at Sailor Jack's Upstairs Bar in Benicia, especially Deborah Fruchey, Marty Malin, and Jim White for their comradeship and critique; Ana Manwaring; the Baby Boomers at Rianda House in St. Helena; L.A. Women's Journal Group for thirty years of inspiration, as well as the late Holly Prado; Dolly Ogawa, Patrice Bousson Barrie and Maurine Doerken for their friendship and collaboration; and the late Marty Shapiro for his encouragement in the first place.

Notes about the type: Snell Roundhand, used for the titles and initial caps, is a script typeface designed by Matthew Carter in 1966, based on the work of Charles Snell in the 1700s.

Adobe Caslon Pro, used for the text, is a Caslon revival done by type designer Carol Twombly for Adobe. She was inspired by the classic letterforms of the past, from early Greek inscriptions of 400 BC to William Caslon's typeface of the 1700s. (An added tidbit: the Constitution of the United States was set in Caslon.)

Made in the USA
Las Vegas, NV
18 July 2022

51714562R00044